THE MAINTAINS

CLARK COOLIDGE

THIS PRESS

This book is published by this press in an edition of 1000 copies. Printed by Maud Gonne Press, Oakland.

Sections were previously printed in this and Adventures in Poetry.

Distributed courtesy Big Sky Books
by Serendipity Books Distribution
1790 Shattuck Avenue
Berkeley, California 94709

Copyright c Clark Coolidge 1974.

laurel ratio sharp or hard
instrumental triple to or fro
granule in award

one to whom is made

nave
bean
shin
spectacle
as the near wheel

of all subdue
a overhang
or bear over as a knot pass
the spread

that fair
the part
of the part plots
ending in for the most part bolts
as of wholes
golds
come to as risen divides

paper a half surface certain salts
such as full sit to the waist
turtle
dative object
flute or the like bonus

soup spindle
cloth ink
pit spring
bones to the axis of the bore to part
holding to do that draft
mar

a pluck comes close to
cones hence or ahead
issue
as or for one dents

humph
that wattled
place over hence
with urchin
which occur in the not true scales
slow green off with blue
more side
also and of those he was suffix

of the clock
note
terminates as an one leaflet
steps
or white person

bid protein
quill in full
lit square flower sulfate
or of another with each other

as a tremor with quoins
game
tape
red bill
also any of several serrate jars
the only place force genus
cause of roll
start from hat
state

or this natural or video
poplar forms meaning coke
envelopes
invert leaves

or more up from middle
blunts
leaves dash by the slip tick
as on

as at which props
a twin
and full agate pass
a jest or the like wad
waff
act in them
as a mote looks on or speeds
whole hence tablets
a double button

coat to send glass
see bill
called a swingle
is so hung as to beat
hence of woolen
lacking and also having
quarts

of flam of extol bean
of using chem
the pea suture inducing insectile
furniture of pole divisions
sending forth with the fold at the top
lens shape back phase
as some one of the nodules
woody and rind
preposition of either
the arboreal mild

a width of the like
most used rapid paste
a small
away or small

between without the mob forms
icing disc-lobed blend
cue tailed
the fried acute

acid
non-czech
also any hours as a chaplain base
after the one to take to not appear against
the painted but having no dim
not one nor one better than none
a state of being the like

intervenes
talc
often noting no milk of the suit lead
to render for sorts as hence
no sort yet left
a disc on the head or the like
one's for a term
repeats cast off spring
sound state in materials
shuns

bleater
the dry hub
to loose or draw
has been like also to be
back or aside
wear or blink
dims and acts

past of blow
blimp one home
blister copper as sap but one
due from ice at tennis
around a cent wind
cynosure
any of a central able carp

dropped
edge of other like
contents that will run out
of several blent
minerals eyelid
to raise in a canon
less flex or more canned hemp
and is much as masses liquidic
canopic
sonorous same kind uranium
dipping which by recipients

row or summons
of being commencement
with a coo or coos
not classed as silk is wound
the coupon
courts in reply to another
habitant
the face of a type

steps also this
as in the mast of a running suit
now only in some set tip running
see court
wholly from the main dormant
broadcast rodent
one shoulders
an amount of the day of the dope
used for does not
fend and right reason
dulls or to the doodle plants
fish

a dime
as the one or that which hums
limb in reports of the tube
kept hulldown
gathers in huddles huffs
cards near the resthouse khan
such as cathode meters a cow
cognate realm
or gradual hollow tuft

stances cover
number and neck
as a part in what one is not
subject
matchlock to a masterpiece
or the like things of immaterial scope
lower journal
mongrel moth or mastic solo

called pole
called made or right booms
a mono or diurnal linen
during life
more name
used of a mountain range

class stone whole course
the string is sounding concord over
angles all holding
or single things
pile right to the handle
nincompoop of nine pips
in motion as a thimble
or formerly in undress

to varnish niggle
a member of any very detail
will to prop india
a flour nipple or thatch lobster
that nips or glasses
those irons to the indulines
program
branch nut

shown by this word
given about the kinds
with numbers as figures spots
the billiard names
ordinal columns of the table
letter

outline against paper tails blotted out
to protrude
ordered up out-of-date as a shine
hence spanning
standing an outward train
clothing to surface the strata
as thrown on building a paper
rhythm of tail planes

silver pitches pounds
pitch as a heart went pitapat
more obsidian than piquant
this genus a public bill
abounding in pith
as in often circular mining a rope
an open state
afix ship

tux
shifts tart species turtleback
heliotrope
the like trend including the return
to common parade spit
a hair as the weight of the lathe will turn
point also from it
a dense tutor
watch or another in any branch
prong cough
withdrawn turnstone
a similar through
as alike as at a doorway
a twin plant

also sets a cartoon
in breadths
or a several one far
a galleon
carpous
small oxygen of that which carried
communes
hence a game shifting cheapest seats
a wheeled sunspot
caroms the minimum
in hue
in nascent strikes like this

clear
also blemish able to certain sorts doubt
enter into either noun
gram or prop close of a period
having strung horizon
nails which see but hard when seen through
chatter-shaped carry the main sentence
the clavicle to the class meal
or year after year poem

facile in diminutives
club-shaped by the great clay highlanders
hence
smooth even from dense spare parts
or the like use of ether aside
stuck by pierce of strip
the adverb to undergo a held scheme
as fit of flaws
as a sonata

a clap with a clang
a fit name of an action open
as claque repose
see leave gloss or a dark place
in the region of the glottic wheat
upon the angle between glide bomb
a glaze motion without pass powers
meat in hue or of low
wanting dull as in smoothness
model slopes globose

in figurative sap
rather than exact
pose
that which flows in prices mouth
innate without
also a fireplace
attributive of astrologers
to back a flower in principle
matters
usually followed by with

to train
in the manner of a vein to steep
in a state of gulf
lodger

having inhabitant percent carbon
participial
root notes of a transient present
saline easily
effects of a mass so as to sense
a guzzle

cold
inroad
insectarium etcetera
a coroner or guest of some other species
something something firmly
not a mean little sense for size
as edge or the inside curve or turns indoors
the angle beside or number as in ten
chemicals usual parts in a plural
to that which sits in pinpoint speech
flat
undone
brain of an agency
a thin part having absence
having only one lean as said of a roof
occurs
or lets

the other past by a jump or jump it
exception the bivalves
minutes less than the usual unit in odd lots
years wandering to pertain or field thought
of a pole in vacuum one gilbert per maxwell
that minced form
off the white and spring of the quadroon
odd tip points to tongue of triangle
telling the whole tone eighth
clock prefix
having a valence of eight

rollers may move the land or be moved on
written also hence roland and oliver also vexed
and barring plates made him of a nephew
rolling into parallel writing a roly-poly
skate or thing
pudding hence a part taken
the entrance beam of the seals
spacious detriment
lighthouse abounding in rocks
into a ball

beam to lay forward fetters
expend or fold laid over or under another
against wind of laundry of laurel
conveyance of middlings or tailings
brier advocates

the small tier at a tea
objects to visive extensions
after the count or later the next count
vitreous as animate mining
that is a growth coat of rat wheat
a raisin elm rate
wet part or class letter
the first bill of word plant

is bred by wrung sugar of X-rays
and an ireland shaped like it
a feathered slag of solvent tools
lower than the wood of this tree
coats
the parent included another in its rock
inert X of the skin
flags placed in front of the china
resembling wood slang
a general novice and naturalist

as of a boss pie of umbles made
a left end shadow one
from rain one from umbra etcetera
a pirate of lord howe's island
an american magnolia

ingot sloth pealed against
not having accustomed the characteristic of
dates being of one mind
dim about the cave or leave louts
without taking in earth the seech
an untie or skeptic belt
the embodied in unalloyed nouns
not conical as art umlaut
heed usual with valve shrubs
paddles

see bend
game to act as cricket
compound of raw dish hue
the orifice or power peer
one of the small or second umbrellas
like bells in large stemlike stance
such as are matters arose through steam
as metals note below
opinion and eight foot wide shout

shade
the miles version currents
river rhine rung that it bring meter
back or away to another reports
alter
and close rust to clothe laws
afferent potato horns in white wines
more or less smaller than the joints on protozoans
higher than rhodochrosite alp wands
call judges in the lower words

so by nul to render bone
allegiance a printer's proof
one who minds bits also to rotate
mood trumps thought to be of a novel whit
hence grouper
to the ankles of which we live
in form water or noting slate
faith pace in diagonal pairs
terrestrial of the nearest land
on the waist or troy weight
original
and trot hooks from one bank
on its point of basin

pipe trope a calumet clayey
piston pitched and serving perfumery
theater below level pox pits
the yucca pitapat against the plant itself
as the bent part or gland extracts
interior makeshifts
concise as select slope at random
dip tooth in extreme reach
or store in a pit

limestone in hue
the cookery seed of this tree
of or pertaining to or like a pitch in size
or mineral aim dark as a tent's
pip robbery or artistic theft

see airplane
the bent patter of a moving dole
that blend to remove the pith from
or to form pits in
so thus or other will be there
to stretch and willow ossetic
long in value as a table delicacy

webbed and locked and bunting social
an arrow ottoman weighing
in voting a shell

saw an opening in osmosis
to roll down the display state
a horn cell
or marriage thing originated veinstone
for a maulstick at matrices
this is not matter near as often
as a sphere a verse bodes
hops horn
pouts to a furnace
lit outside of a work

saw as on a horse of a meal
notes scope delimiting enormous bills
thigh and height
field of haircut in personnel
a turk times that of the sun
wears the gib
a tomcat

any wheeled bets
if gibbous are convex
to scoff get a sentence
got him in the mouth
get my hat pen box hence
has got to do with have and had
with adds to gain
a semifluid ghee
a used zen for the purpose of same

a face curve hooks
a G I apparatus visible to the magician
as the desert to an accurate and fairy ring
thermometers common salt
coil bunches
as linen
as absolute bars temper

the facts in order of the sides of one's friends
of a coherence crust lacking sequence
presses as a dye
poses either
either deeply or as much used as shingles
striking small portion as a dabber
to wave with sudden peck
a barrel of a pump
or plump circle

scarfskin
unite on the end of edge or flense
that certainly or not
timber of food
scape upon whose dial
a silent by scene by taking up
in the next down beetles
that skimp or conduct a trap
for typing by
a mantle or scale yards
cap

one who aground principles
of this coin the gourd family
formerly automatic written small
the grade cup but now also a slope
attends in top form also rectangular rabbit
containing molar become the voiced stops
just consonant as runaway to gridiron
colorless lees
eyelet aspirates

I bear gishness
a bet and baser niter
mica bars below slight crest
philharmonious to word nouns
bacon lazarus and flumes
in adjectives meaning and bearing
quite white below the typical seals

having a sun used for molding
also as a sodium
strings tongue off the allophone
branch
resin
then fled

that which is zeal wanting in wan war between warbles
manner
something meaning chiefly of cardigan
rug shell yields oil
winter also pear
wing of a cover prison
often forms dentine of a closet
having ware body
minute spark get by ends
show also titles of elk
saddle footing
out of house
said of a stomach

now rare
the fast cohosh by nun under nutlet
algae handles and a base
hence cutouts
gelatinlike
cofferdam
to cave in to cause to neck
to borate
flocked in line stem building stir
chord-awful
bab planes also axis deer
one of any small pointed oats
a state hyperbola avuncular
as greater than any of its anchor
babble circle of this pair

one of the beard
over or before baby palm
rocks over single-bits
situation unhandiness
spinose as crape inside ski
admit benches to well up
come hence akin to will
mass to shaft loosely the air
lot weir
sunday through friday during hat
from one end weekly
water multiple with a wedge
as a thin seats

the woof
larvae of the woofs
tenth tin boxer fixed as bore
finis of a noun to contemn
bone charges of pea merit
cate
to remove tell from in detail
of what is to render supports
a set away leaper measure
as the one or beneath one's harsher
meal for a stop particular
item by port minutely close
the spoonful for one's picture whole
to leave down upon
an act flat

duff of light hammers
given higher but an octave blunt
chair of about the same octave floor
pudding phrased in a bag
hence the date in a charge
palimpsest
making pales the same when read
others set in a close rowed backward or forward

the fur of race history
parts on a needle fluke or county
geological again
click deficient of an individual
fan in some specie
chaff in any pall
zoo cover of being palmate
a wooden rock perpendicular in war
of notions in a close row
pertain
house and the like

song in a former one
made inane of vanilla
an appraiser
changeable when the sail sets not chicken
valves
currency and possibly nitrogen
of sound by color services a thing
not a thing between vamp and patch
vidual instance
the front as place or those baggage
with staff magnitude by winds
at dipoles stray linen pigment
benzoin cord by van dyck

moot common vetch
ozone mosey at the tips
the exactly right rapid moss pink
softened in grimace said
also period
on one's it to spring
that bugle now off pupa
an amounted setting
machine shaped gem
to prompt like edging
shrub if eaten
warp toots bank

express palatal
police mould for clothing marble
places quack camphor

a motley
or loose morning pug
the wool paper swung peen
bill and distensible guitar
storage behind bubble of a ventilate
once held as perfect through spectacles
skin due to some concrete action
bling yarrow
shell of feather as little ball
plain from a fixed point
fired upon the open bill
a skin used of words
striped or flowered as quartz of a suffix
slightly of a crevice as mammal
ing down in front

that god with us in partition
of another object next in line or state
having no voice part of the copy
pinnate to enter in on at rest
the rest of a given period pound next
insect so long as most of the rest as well
area of another like tile
gin mobile
mind embosom
bower to unite in on as radicals
projecting over being fluid wedged in flight

a night nine
the lesser the wax dogs its stuffs
or eggs the intentional candles
as of lamp
international also the tree itself
of the spurge family black
a topped minute near in bone

the canna seats
a shine-hard common
so-called boat tooth of like shape
from the rolls
on which hue a saturation is secured
as a candle about the mouth
mosquito cans stated limes
recorded off the bark or mummy
overhang to sing
a fine coal
or book list of good mass or omen
mustard simple
uses clot in another machines
pie star sliding
a perpetual vow

bart
bolo bar sinister
bolsters control for dropping
optical woolen
melon or a round
at low bond
of a wall of the table
or a deep atom wind means
red cap neap row
large service entry running cotton audit

booed often tissues supposed to revisit
a thread bass to figure the cathode
does on one inch
slight for the complete that which is to film a novel tobacco
a minor bronze ribbon of the body
of the hand one inch to the feet
thumb
vary bowl as on a piano
engaged in breadth of whale gem states

hence with falling in on a large scale
to one who or that which fills
a sum of motion to as water fingers
name attains a length of sixty feet

spar based on the collective skidder
to which is it
as fine-tooth as ordinal growth
of a filter proper as a dumas
find such linnets as read book
comb to search through small posts
the sake
flat out in the brain
the capital for foot mark motion
the ball man

conglomerate aldebaran
still roy in the eye
off the shadlike stamp
served hence as a thin loophole
to the appointed arms in monazite sands
the bot cup still on the lead look
out set dish by dish
stamps having a wing
alcoholic even though all through
airmail a pump
airhole larded in briskness the less
in there envelopes gaze pass
each to a stated ring
the judge as to both and loss
having a stated pick of such nouns
are as used by turners
fencing is in effect
full-length practice volume of prolong
still wind cone as a distillate cleavage
a stop matter
the period of time

moting into leaked out occurs
made with or having no
leaves with or which see
hood
through ing or using barm
or undone a marks tree
that the lead rests
formerly only when are leap
real lead of a top
a folder mean
and hay by some to about
to jog as in a wall
connect
a bound or octave
ushers in in probe inhalation
which into use wave ointment adverb
past parts twine
direct lower thriller with bands
in much like horno quartz
twin tubs blende

aluminous
of a wasp and the whose
often used nutlike cloth
hair on shipboard
mound in dim to make one
a large hence such wires
either as somely spotted
with two fit char or tubule
of in shape doxology
or light lamp as a bit
in room color plum
cord or the like yard
in step out cloth
later wall from state
gag pledge with its foot
a misgiving salt
to zinc that that comes cliche
rent

gaited
fair as in line card
to swoon value slope
stitches drudge into factors
wind
a small
to deter clear detrain
agreeing
to scatter record in fish
an adherent right poem
blow
capping phlox as in alphabet pinks
panding
to stem openwork cyanide
women with reflexed apex
leads or tends
concurrence gases
chat cone

pan and med
orchis
slipper nucleic payee
thing
side with but an R
one hue in era
to form as small fix maple
orbis see utter group
isinglass
floats in air that of others
as much of mouse
triglyphs meter
water or chem suffix
jurassic rightfulness
jut length kappa
slang drawn in
heritable gymnasia
gadabout asbestos

striped being poundal
a foot of the stock daytime
treated of the dado
rapt to sent takes point
otolith
ant in electric eastward
adhere the sensible horizon
complacence optics

legume
to be read to celerity
lowering one or who that
one which
is just warm seas
earths
having these parts so in
in fee like gauze
taking on a tackle frank drink it
rendering uniform
plants when the sun is cross
in open board
setting knob in a direct as
soon as one or whom
ionic volutes
even way in the states
woolen leather water seat
tween as lack or want matter
grades
without only in
one of noise barbules
the case of the tube of the body bar backs
from handles it lagoons
now only in name or hill
the watch thing whole

ordinate two the tree
me in shortest azurite
similar into
being to come notices
a wall hanging in bad hence
cause tude
aperient aside or bees
in an otherwise
choke
nothing aniseed notes means london
an a one
oleoresin intention of plus
formed in one also mere forms
cesium allegro of type alkalai
such coterie from him the bill
platitude
departure of being monotint
trust sepal or poem of one
it my lord buff bring
which yard travels
is drawn upon it was once
name cap in pack bowls
blotting
out or to be verb or lack
table also acts press
in as much as so far is
it ins and outs but an if and or no

toft use in meterage
or on place the ture or substance
of the staff of any rock
medica lemon timberclear
port parts to limp
sour tupelos of open-chain sheep
one who lines back up another part
by or borders

beam chief of lime
siegfried calyxes
furthest one of act from
grapple lead grain
pitch brings to the fell
denote flamer resting cells
spoon rise in fifth foot
rata nish with spoke
that is in poll rabble
thumb marine suss
one versal clip milkwort
gadoid in orchid much
register or pollock

shorn gala milk
mend jargon or U.S. footpath
in a patent pounds
lighted not heavy
a chunk lump in comp juts
number rush by junket
wick out or to
ways with of
polyhedron of ichneumon
putting green
lining quartz
short tube or bush
print spore in a boat
antlers ferro iris
see same

one of a size
a gap or under coverture
hypothetics of a churn
bird wound like a dart
parts to set off telegraphy
avow simpleton adhesion to
clamp type of sugar
cat also its fur

detail parts with barometer
legal or expression
in a group war flat
dite ton one
one underbound ponds
grace bone

madras and and an miles
stone any is of often
such
often overall trasted
matter in usual to or as a
also skill hence lens
for a part as first a clothe state
so to his seal
lantern maybe
view lath also of speech
cannot
or last lowed joist
an upon string
dent care
act of protract
boxes given fair hue
whitewing carbonate blank gloss
any of lead chess
prop of who wane
fast a loose
fid croach no-wave

bling plank
that is a surge pence
prob roller act
overt broke bear
ness pitch
hemp while
nate nant

ing or pare
in phrase not all beer
in slanting to slate
time an unshirt
a mopartment
fogey former
in the like of
the first which often
certains ocarina
meteor or oboe erasure
prop gusting
mucid or elsewhere
misses presses
wind the plant

either wimple
or with heaves
thong syllabic
use until so
trigonal fuels
to cam at feet
schistose alike
in thus the waltz

whorl caudal
done by or gone
slight to grounds
sur scoter
said of a rope
point in goad
tort ascent
rob bur marigold
check now as sing
warp a stale
an air fast

ployee eyelets a spect
mottos input the like be
couch ace quincunx
may to calm
goes brooch pines
out the uke pinks
rent to such a disc

shell surface a patent
mint test for kneepan
grants
labroid as a word
a sharp
to hence a crush
valence it

jurassic form
case
mood
gram
a true jut some
pure edge cash
am here here I
versed use for matted use
alphabet each other title
lands as just ago too
bent fill a line
saturn is roofing

hep into vaunt tends to acute
airless-suited
the been heritor
done to shade with
lar gown
deck geniture
mason rather toggle
two pad
the polar same equals

ing it thus in
treme
ma-ing on ouzel haploid
gist
pitch
farm blocks to sheet
to such see of
or on in
estrone insult
noun pine onset

the end cent lobate
glance while gum
articles block lead
hemmed salt opts
with and act have spoke
pand render egret
sight as radiolarian
as might poses past
in boards in ton

turtle or as needs plant
a thin is term gel
prices list tooth
tristram monitor for salad
varium low
lave avalanche
pout
than cambric
apposite
even surface
phonetic one who or that

index bark
little being
just another motile
the bivalent
that prop

state ist
beadsman purse crab raisin
dome stitch

in still blocks block of block
blocks of pin stain very

somethings
bat of elgin
the more morris andle
a grass pectoral as graphic granite
a cut clear mean and not as granny
mass kind of mirror
aged and crushing and finds bills
tip an N
woody minute as cannon as grape is made
bars plan and are the active
about like that of a single
cell bears

calculus braces suspender
gamebag or organ in
branch in a race repair
fusing high hat grain wheel lock
water bulb of leads to cheese
blocks class with air as the fir

to an end
end
to arms small boils
fleet a red silver
charm on or upon
boding lived
north of back a little after
first in
now eagle
three hole
earmark on

card another
third earth in order
wages note yards

list born on
delay as nouns
one making one of paper
eighth zen
crusta
domed to deal reap
its dentoid curt in short
a vogue drawn by
idiom comb
drub

coin path of branch cream
make
or matter to a liquid
type see ant

hue in of tree dial a pod
age code time or ball with another
cod to a proper close
lands of cake egg strut
snail rung at no two
to bay
the verb to toupee

rail depth said of colors
arc agent of inch
heel hence piece
bowing plea grounds rolls
platyhelminth applauding such unit
of so as to of
nose stage
a sheet tree

plate
of course
game from agent
course or use
ance
span cant
mails steer a chem line
carbon cherry radical chevy
to wind in case
address
pronoun hence
overtime either or
stow owes
ore shoot set
top woof
singer placing carbon

nihil that isn't
so of its niche
a white still hence
to leg it irons cheese
palm leather etcetera
middle parti-pressing milk adder
this thin which both
very it is met worth
farads or other it
fluence setless

arch kit
with once quality of verbals of bodice
times the forms annul
lose from those in full
or coil other of soon as point
to pertain twin having bufflehead
febrile or full or one
obtuse deck the means
back

diamonds to be
when more there are disc
letter it in actinic stamen
cloth to spring lingo
doubles due office or the like
keeper hence
dock tail
raisin chiefly nucleus
parts or may not
boot with a few
pet cosy as an angle
stapling a german

to sorts that binds on who stands
apple civil and when
ding sail left right
risk of an out below
camel
eyelet
wingspread
having been found into the had find

ball coin
routine on another by wheel
trails light an often as biscuit
said turnip on disuse
proofs pronounce a clam to
taste of taste to

again to lease to have to load again
of a past upon of one's hand
another having
late of a mock up answer cell
fan hind ground
the right in lands
water table matter beets of hen pith
certain as how the elevator
while place or paper stage

pugs
to pull upon as to pull as to
of which
no noun

one kneel is read
of rest stated deserts
of pieces of use as N
fade flat or see gift
fag end thing to been
thermometer tog
shining or not to act hearing
wanting dim

the ism one ables hair
dish in ionic calyx
coarse as gird sing up archies
upon vests another
mitts alee ratio puts
off drive hide earth
imply
the outer toward with also work
ting part of erasure
oxide as notes space

tic topiary
suit of mast
parts of a topaz few
turvy straight such by surface
tops upper soils by rig
feet long now like
clicks up among
a small which the ball is
the ball is an

bone skin pitch with
tone don't
an down trifle in its

as a sea
one an thing snapping
snark hale

a junco
as in the term of its score
can species
to block with
and and
or paid

it casts
notch
scoop in

plant degree of adult stage organ
given as at after as of a
short
or in return
felt manner

peregrine utter
by blue B by salt A
place to place
forelegs strong in light
help is the like
oak of row waste
an oatmeal thin
in pictive minus
subject to infinitive
needle want

end at one end rod
a roll to veto
one done with must
a voltaic
certain aphid tube
less by a half major
biscuit rocks

the first and third half pert
minor a child's interval
oligocene league
a locust short
film hole at bay
with a lock
nut
lay or deposit

for use ton
locus limes
rat state metal
gas as wooden
flume by beverage
cent
linen aid of lips
fat the cup
chap for sale

milk to the right
a let
means over feed
up in store
to duck calls to encroach
outside in nib invert
a sap as has toes as to hinge off

to insert
well as to center of or intend
the bema
kind of the cell
to hide pent

Some zeolite or chop
hulot lands
sides
in full bear
now in top out
disc sleepers or ties

handle horseness
full side with a cat
boast pore slug in grill
rigged often on garnet
meant was
as is meant

swan's
deck as fish
on one sides both wear
some put flag
flag from a render come
lid but
chalk like
in sphere an equal
bow a back on
hold of another
ohio river

east rare earth
pods it and all
of scale forth
seal still wife
discus
brakes to train in
on as one radios
or gave also up

walls in cargo to vent up a view
that is that it is
content sounded
flood prop to hatch slides
table it to flavor
a gross hollow
down

toroid deltaic
springing each unexpand
sonar to sound
teeth away
pass greatly undue
or disclose

partition act of plant wrongs
scot eye deck of septum
shunt of bony any of a taper
dike cone dim
fit for a like digit use
seeks and zools
losis

common the common which sure
lime fit to repose
any parts clack
jujube skis
to part chopin mark christ
gill clefts mary baker clarinet
one of dupe gull or truss
chops chroma selling at

aspic cheep
sheet in alms
grows chew
ice so as to spot letting
cairngorm salmons grisaille top
to or a curb
groper borage
rectangular rabbit
ing whole
tret
ment
oins

grocer grocer
cero at pintado
sideways
throne boards outer by-line
sieve express
bill of chicklet
ab initio argentum
mate at met center
joke hole sunk hole well
as you are
weight akin to wen hope
weighs
pearls weeks

from as to drip
black will alkali
pal rafter hypoblast
force of face the lacquer turks
lag to it
keeper of onca
jags vanilla
yields
brung the wicker
shrub
prick

jade an upland lath
to out by a tire
sired signals
interscapular
among other bran
troth adduce

can may being
mantid
cap of being motion
jut this but in may
polite it as a drub
at full math length
to get as does

breech
face
a disc at right face
house gorge
dim longs as a hook
turn through or pass by in
aqueous outside adjective
the blip potatoes the make
wind

circles forcing or series
plasm of to cloud sully
not echelon
ness black
a minute neigh
bivalent knickers
ketone ornament
wasly drupes
various as the large

tide for pay
hemp members the coal
scars iodine
of one keep of being so
cathode a going down
it a it

main to milk cert keep
edge the after keeps well
steels hence mantra shorts
mail matter to set push
as a as a note

tamp
only in which is to be as
drake arbutus perhaps
in red perhap gloom
a veneer by lying
rent of air

overrun
overhence
tuba than an a bar
rinse
surface

gainer indwell
lifts form base
by a cause to be parts
been one chambers as own
coerce bias dog
not and cease
takes just only in also

crease as bulb
one in

hats a book
about as spin
shins that prawn hastur
mono flies cow
genus saw bent
saw met sound

flump deck as a flush
with to had
tone meet
foot per tone met
with with age as fluorine
by or as if by
be to prime any hence bolting
part up of flue in the weight
bung mix of imp
a bot
genteel falls by rupt
cow now shirk
to now to an end
or want of or

in place of sit or hold also of part
likes give rise of
that to take
as in of it
to cooper
dite
to it the like tastes one
ing by as teem
to one as to one to back
to acts dimes
a such test
puffs block
as such as paid stern

whole cleave in sticklike gamble
fact or let it is to stet fing
alcohol of a matrix server snore
arm pose spore by piercing
atom paper or check knot
terminals chin silt feminine
a sulfa occur
daub damp smoke globose mint
smallish as cement in peace
slab mints scent

a trunk down
short in program aced
rant at sight
soon that is as to be
iron as red
leaf pent by safety french
may to can small hay pelagic
arch in some way
pelvis rest of the shoe
of it made

means to lay by two last post
organism of helping
depiction table to a liver
to also place
a letter to other addition
ale loose hence beef
chalks a misser
account of slag sheet bulk
consonant
allot
biking

snood hive
sown arbuthnot
cling each
alba nice
a crimea
teal lunging
aisle a pant
barmy sled
annealed polite
garred
seem a kite a newel
don't

bump dice a latch bases
crimpy seeds alight
a scone colt
mere wristy
idler A B C
tumbler cease
it
ice at
it seems as coils
bounce end
it els
armiture

blimpy
cone axe vinnegar
ore lem peas
stem X
of lifts budger
sud

put that it is sent top also pawn
a race of is then
or an to as as in
under for to part or the like it
patent on which as the
and a spelled follow
archaeopteryx for keep means
the one and prop to out lily
hydrolysis twigs salix

one of bulbous now others
dam into or fig to con out
times ear as in
cendent form bone
like bone of pulp pick
as in mineral or evince
ossian and dial
use often as if
led if
in of
out it
of tion or out from
in as out a
into from
not other as elsewhere
otitis ways
fid ob
a solvent mem bluish

a bony to take a
bring put
non as which do not dim
no said done can in more
used ting in give
an one to a suit
gerund of of
particular half as a loaf
with the co-op cap mid join lift
an one nine sides
cuticle nones extent a lawn cap
nones

pronoun notes not is
fermendable belong
a long that of the
velocity borax
chops graph borage
shoe tree hence nor dotage boppist
phenol other of two sheep
carded from through use
stems mute due be
with a stock a gas idle
a flat rust

been
said of with must any of
ratio or who that which
stops as lodge
act spot
bread of mass use sand lob
boiler only pale to that
an even as even confine

octa-hawser predicate
head for as of a poise
boxing up moths
sack verb when nears

something to that low by something
kept or stems a net
in have as had it at it
march in high tone
over have under as one
the oat metal as sound one

on the left house
niobe bowls hand shoot nips
niggard jot to cut chip
gifts in close
neh
dis
cheese
happen lasting
motto of gown bolt
pence clamp space in C
on the pop be of cons
peony
penult to a stamen melon
sort that's slate
obtainance such
concrete than now

ring reed
sugar umpire
freed ebb
aim and less less
reflex set flux pulse
tries by calvin
again or front
keepling pleistocene
eye bun

calyx
mantle vein
or bank a
husbandry put place thing

labels are long by
one's lot or of
issue through peer
a formic squid
tea made any all see large from
card bill
thing hole

back down in front
in range vase
dashes of mines
toady dine gland
part chase in half or half
tissue like as with
herb copy of picric cattle
living no matter as what copper
sphere that which another
other
cloth math one

dull sought to baffle
an un but is to pcr
who
certain in verb log a felt
of in not any not
deck
re
ing of
a joint ness
oppose of manner
basalt a mirror
plan pin

hydrogen a warble shake
a three fish
ant
flaps end

having year colors
used near one for and
as of a woven having
catch bay
once iamb in iso-barking
fork prismic tire
room in a scot
a minute or very blind small
utterly tint to wheel
with blow mix in than
a fit pan kite tin
hat a sheet giving
as from row bar numbered loud
very above the long tall
to rope grown and said
on one's it hue and abbot to be slate

arsenate at cast control
herb mump warp hemp
placed pit of the pit
a land to
abreviator a tenure blimp bridged
grounds in on earth pinch for terms
a moola tate that next catch par
below or esteem
bead drag whale mill to tips
suit head
horse awn

past in taken the most and like
ing hair
being as the than by which things
may thing by
will it off are
of cause are
or one to one to as
a train hold
place none

wood sateen as a sack pride
surface polo's sat in cod in
onyx parts for twill bosom
must a man in the leg
pilchard silicate by sappho
a bush see sard
where title beams an eighth
which full log and also table
with a use by the pliers
lish
in dwell not cap act

rolls well wads none
as through
a bill from composure to hawk said
recoup hamlet minus take off
buys one pewter are that portion
such of ceding back
to like from being
reptile from and no more
staff primrose

stopple
straw con asthma
straight port first whole
on rooms set of floor
a short of others sand large
half whether left also for it test
half green upon either
osprey who as a given to one
alga certain separate
examine lines slight due
more hence than is half basso
map shall occurs
of out bit
as jocose beat drupe
hurry left after teeth
as if at

braic juice tell
leg slight due
for in long be stay
veto or plate maths
often of or often to
to it as adds or likes
universe tend lace
ton zool
scopey berlike plastics
lambent
gill a pitch
whack to lager law
wove papes
landau cuts rolled hotel
are so brimmage

kick as pick resinoid
make state fit outs
spin noun ing
devoid pad
freight water ash mean
french hind nutria
barbal hood
as eggs who won
to ones
slated next as any clothe
clip mal cousinry
nail now both sweet
than gain uraninite
is of it close cloots
bot
gog
vary

hazard pen come unhap die as
set of sum's due
in hair anyplace bowls
bluffs

laced bort
antelope bugles past
some or entrance float
coal bung borough cock
from one's what is forms
poach tarp any as red
vary bear
hydro lily equi-parallels
stalls one drills opera
also as in a been
wooden single on arm star
tick

dent or in the list close
motile
sequences if bolden
or out of lack of out or also
embosom
bud of said as said tin
all the mo
god
olio iffy
grant
every tube surname to miss
ties grant of grant
a holly

pelvis crossness
infer out adduce polish
by erase of lack a planet
gram ad limit
valid char
ferrous nether
indwell
varia lancet
effable nesium region fictive
caliph jut

sworn
cut so as to parrot
sole note esker
bet kappa choirmaster
as sulfate almost
jerboa-like burr
hills

plaid low
often sphere
object tea
may
that causes is plural
roll
cell sieve
from-horns
who
traffic-pub
bivalve odor shoe an oddster
botanic eight
ostrous sextant
matches that
numb
ock
than-text

look an ogle
cipher of all-set
troop
taft dog
a shun band
the so-part close
mark stomach
chestnut awning
sung
marbled and profit

mantle the few roots
by moon
squilla
book bling

many plies
cotangent
now a tell
infra-anal
local with air as tense
longer called a make
of tufa a top hind
the like
it rains up holds
on the inter-pomp
ruddy opt

solar strike
tag frank
genus iron quarry leaves
a from
a hob
a say from
bottom in
bat that suits hits
hook of trick
latinous
robin and thing
newt as still whoa
hoak
a hither
a matrice

nearest as stop
as some
and thats

from clause
itch
alba obs
of two of the of too
and grivet
adds made
has as under its
index out
a grim as get
got
to pen so
as to
privity pleat aid
orderous
fan twine chose
a chose
ting full adept
hue-color

hour
plies
as bad ample
desdemona bend
plastic full
also its nouns hull
ratio yule
arm owl
bean stat
dune
piano in what dune
geo-piano bodily
a mitch
logs all pard mains
mean
mean

bout what boot which
a nascence is of its over that's
nine eights a told
what sown as at the which its
the ban fat sun tools vimmer
taints
lasting can'ts abates
boning at risen stills
arc loads
lodge
ilk

ammonites as stasis
donut lights tab laves
sum mega-with trump eggs
dewey
doing bring the time with
open lights with the limits thrum
docent there
grip which's dock
or short a male family
totter film or
diorite

lower sights thru opening sinks
to slope in sud
tents of something gas read in
deck to foot the part pairs
twice or feet less wings
stop up a dip salt
long
some

maya many cover mere
with against to place in by set way
doing a lid sport with less coasts

paging drones
come met
refers rasp scale to diatom
spun or galled place
as skates top then rays box
herbs file by crack parts
here as lot glued to fill
rationale sing

a bid result from fall bulbous
spikenard ample of it
adds at it
pamby plenty than nile's sake
the tude host
to derive peel
tune off with discs all
sailors mean paints
more of any piece alike
a crock sow dupe a gull midst
scale wound as scale act
a par glass as faiths

like a so enamels peep
recess nones in fact
of loaf to not any
to iron
a hence an adieu
lean
an out's an in and times it
copes

lear
to not it's to what it's
for not it's found what it's thus
peaks

annulus
three fours time limp flies
are made
design of of whose points in
open fume of time lots lowish breach
trees from one
bounds for beyond
to lime which
as ortho-rhomb syllable of a pearl salutes it
                             solutions to pen iris
the bow
ants bull
into's to in

in that made to such or to speech
that applies is said to be one
hog fold full wasp
less but less on to see at
chart part or other of statics
or one on a sup more
wield ends done
intro hence of the arc
with con sum by cast one
not within be or not to

master in only bore
is march
plant near moon toward haste
spring undue now more
as ease in free from stand eaves till
diamond cannot stamen
the diaper to fence
igneous to its dialogue
to a dim as the steam to divide
point boxing an arm scales
set on

as which as to set up
beneath the
into eggs not put as a post
oil in article jews that will
ridge
pent

points one to two of gas
pack on others the air on one
purple or the like of its kind
rubbers of long brings
to give off the take of the over of some
rod spell stick a fox
to post turn as lose
a form fit from
beverage hence pleistocene
notices behind use a name to notice
are out of dick's hat
as with of
and his see
the any the are so breaks
lime and
set call pose
port and

every as last pent some
addle binds as
as somewhat a day a tin
lad at sand bow
a stem latchly a curé
gone's left tune suit
tensor dispatchly
over a twin a send handy wheeled
condite
ore oboe pinnish

done as can
nomad of sulphite
uppon cabbage as space to all
acts jet prints just
right in or right mean
whole so as to
the one's the in to one
of fond into hole
like rest which sees
index that slag
duals in wide
tea saves
ort ones

scaleboard
an oriole more match applies
having wholly
with to meet join to come
or it adjective hair
land of nearly series some
of it so as to it
the almost form of
the right right

timer a table as keyway
and light be begun by related
high that the minute is an one
of full that walls note
out also the passover will
craw
any king
type the boxthorn
metronymic as coloring
in math one versed
a jaw from off his game
point of off

oxide thought unit organs lyric
word negro paces from a place
vehicle from meaning
zinc for play
from shell of fencer
sphere slightly herald
and evince
in order for hard out of order
backing
one each into one like

flat for cooling and the one
lay set
in one's as one's to back in
just a state but many
as in color small or another
near as the word also to that
such as only
the result that
water one

part due rock its own
acute to thin school leaves
such as mouth and which must be
thin or as
to all offs
piano papers
things by others root
be notch whorl
salts from it boast
gaskins in braggart
wood or ball spar not a gap
to see to chat

rope east also card an east
due sea decay the ocean
first full in state vase
both tarp bias
part point a group worse
part any hence sex
as lawn pen pump chop swell mend
stub roof

hydroxide
vowel sans stucco top
boulder web till the linden stall
subjoust as wheat used bill stall
note help
bolt more dial
latin tilt

when thing of the same was there are
convex mean
dent to their add
one cease in state of most one
peas often shoe mild race maps
neutron quitter or the like a lot let up
of skate to its album that which
gain having able into chloride
hencehold polygonum
in one other much a craven
about in the use in still cheese
as above of an one

temp period no part shows
cord phrases boards
a slip diet flue chin
jut
cabbage slang bantu sulfate
whom and burlap
as cup as a tax

at a made by with to the add
part hence to both tie
but more all to its which one
one's widely like
the which by like thing means
some pass come dim of falcon other
that lack to open spots
stick point in god
ohio card

strict widely and both all by
of a formerly part to loops
lead side type by block ring
fib or in lose
with the of after ever idle
scale snow
in or point
obs faults
chief or last parts
thing or of its furnish with hence
or as if with with or of ink
been
triangle words an usher
level as in both of state
dunk
of will reduce
usual other same as is
gear by O
one or that one of mine potato
twin to dies recapper dido step

brill or choice
dicentra chimera
pile green groom card
dite brig
or like of to things that butter
as the tried over cycle ether

dultory vert
usage
quilt var
a wood tow in con
owns one's out
pertain
gem step

blanker's a well well two three
fair or fire as as to as
much hence front
do pun
an trim
one such
forth or pass go as nose
the or but the cocaine certain
anew a likely such as noise
surf duck it leans hang
tim base
lacto
a freight was tic um

leather out least the half as made dog
read tended with made or times
the leak in or out as must be pitch
frogging lean
rose
form a chart heath larder
mean garnets dim in hue starch grand
grand through citron
type fulgurite pluck
use last part long
on which long of same some
diameter dicker
id grebe

tap
day one it airs
wire cook
point curling
buff death
score wash
smolt
to feed as to box
helm pint
jack
apt

one akin tetra
wrist
by will nautilus
wyandotte
coat mix
finds in also light
bow apt

casts add of letter scot rock
by table not cap
deserts to one's one
yam boom
gap out
pith its noon or end
a wen hope lots tack
wednesday with and
stopward the lapwing
been

growth stow
in one of a put and short
all been most
rayly pitly
any like as awe which of that
stitch sponge pound
sat blip
been door none

ofs
mild but both
singer doing sake kind
follows nip glass
a beneath nickel
wink plate nodular gus
torch garsh
who one that is
lambda
timber

rope with keep that won't side
block golf that fills
wool coal to coin finds
skid used felt
concave lean blow sum
it held into as large
by hone lower grosbeak
lettuce a handle hence
a mute took foots a grain
ceiling slighting
breech levees on
part to sent to made rose as
up a sealed dye
a let lack of of

point bubble puma over
mostly discs as a class vent
beans tire
a thin as an a centrum
someone that or as what is
back being good
refrain to each ends
lowish-red a scape another
climb bake scales
less like to next stocks
gram from view

a spur abaft
birds back obstacles ply
a faint gourd mental

governor date
tops snap
dill coin mitts step
anode a tart
dull be to part feet
bank a bank mathing cold
betweens sieve
a kind of eat to knot a shell
buttons rotter
gem rose

any bias to cap
amends tenable
ginning class
web mode plates pitch
cards belong another
a call as bill
ester bowel during like land
term beat
dress as bird
word as bill

of while let
a lit yield
ear stones of eight lines
other precedes
one often will as in contrast
uranium use in chewing
club per mass
ball for coin
einstein one in numeral
soda large
fault as unit rubs

presses for shrub booms ring
macaco
word cake broken by packing fop
lobe
verb doctrine cells letter
amend choice lymph bay
becomes one with its one seems
bobcat harp dispersal
class shaped sap as jut
dulge

just takes mean act done
grant out axis
maze being slug in posse
tide at length
utter rockers
puck robin thing
with with
tydol hocus goal chat
sometimes which as that is all
cylinders some book

knot hobble collide by him
a move tissues a pitcher hive
woody grape
high low accord stalagmite bars
nurse contains biotite
soft or lead
a runic fur lifelike
fur thief spring
a bulbous forks tin in seal
bow farthest
lycee pant
of of

pawpaw tumult
cigar of a shock of an ore
rag stamps fit pan
lieu of a palm
resting the shrew sheet nebula
tonic roams
tallow of the greeter
hydrous in full great go
to dock peso aluminum
table rotary sac
pertains beam like speck
bean
a traduce
leaves bread a blade mote
alexandrine pin
cubics his hence
ganoid lemon
which tolls a rate cut
tommy tone cuts
over larvae a stoke
a tassel stock

rootstock shelflike mallard
shellac also dog tent
left twinner sugar
upon which measures a din
convent reflex bobolink
wind concrete
hydromel acumen is on
notes or rests yards
stop leaped fat that is
a barm
broad leave lick stoops
term a given base
extramarine
ablative twine of

for the fade use of smart mined mode
firmly in fast by act do another
plaster link phrase to protozoa
hawser of tie adipose
wealth spun ant lean
tire vessel top score
flag hind such as vole
interval side in such field more
gottlieb blenny

cell rain colors display bear
emit trim so as mar
wood its with
long of had for whose
scud the like
names weight
have to use
as light cold tube stripe stout
vowel
roof twist solid
knowledge over hackberry
isolde triturate
neat turn a cock shirt
lime sleeping stringpiece
pass one's pace

on one's hue slate
means by two main pent
still box one cooks
postulate pastille
openchain any ohm
bland is like verb it is
in become salts leave
belt glacial wire opal point
often gym brook

wide as zero letter
having bearing mustard or disc
silver with you
zarf sonant
as period of part noun yourself
newmexico sign of ceiling
footly highly figures
roentgen of the thickened
wriest crab hazel
dents per paste
volkswagen said of wool names charge

folds to gray and squeegee
quell storage ranged
onion being
that in older was own near
crush to open
module cornice later any
gram by umlaut
radio nor too little
and some in link pose
than as that
tawn vend

attribute wind in tempos pile
peas shoe a mild
rose slang
matzo copper
mat beatle member theory
as hoax as an ash
text that light of done
marge suffix
outline
coil pulp

one such also out of column
loppy
light street teeth sail
mass of view means of words land
inshore fossil tuft of gelatin
bud cranks and objects poem
ray par of the con
to coat gas in glue pay treat
from colonial to form
a skier making tacks
shirk they car
and back and flue seal
bon funnel collog

antiphonal chondrule
snap trust toxin
as not as for gram at all
swage blocks rosin ekes
usage image or figure one magnets
rubber meaning of object ball
table is of hip like knack
arty as of tin
lines dye
spoken whose sung
mouth both alums

end to do with as
apart as to be set
molasses arrow stunt boiler
gather with flood bottom
used bird to fade fries
nouns that microtome
mosey prolix beget
ravage furnish
rates one or rates braid
over sit by bill

rigadoon calcium
from verse right to left run
spike spherical dull
the less the like see stop
thew saw west math
futura undermost aqua golf
mine wade under bat
bonus through
corollary milk way poles
show 'gainst
manilla to a roman pear
to each size teeth
mesmer circum merino
pod botch spare one
used indian
denotes buttons
books any one of having a line
pencil graver

island among peve reverbs
part for adjectives
ishtar of organ lack not bolt
europe found on house bunch
also more whom of wile sac
fobs
staying sand close prolong
dorian else
hide embark abate round
deck deck a couloir
prob
a cake pet
that that codes
cotton well breeds
chord agate like cats

belonging to slow the means day in the period
of a tree a book as by the stretch to right
milk legitimate legs
or of a group long or on side
invest having
eleventh dating filling a contents cabbage
takes verse upon bluff
in point in any column contracts
treat
whole give take such
on teach dash crust blips
incrust loft bay
genus spoon as underwide
imp in as let me hold one
nose with fence open zero
goop each lag freight
either a triangle on facer
rope leaves iris

right tourmalines
right make sun when
thus dust cash whose
province to due fly
impart lasts
dwindle cork a baring
branch and member potter close
of the middle lobster
who keeps keeps it is
frame wear

panicles
one
from
one whole
from small well to tin still
pound one's tries this

    epiblast place plaits
    who with
    part those
    with of
    certains
    in or chat see
    back on as talk
    to which long
    plaque perempt
    osis
    piece also a no
    also such in use
    diet out type
    a none bells
    green at yes
    jambeau
    foot to sheets cap tables
    the any more
    lathe
    prep the like
    ambit elbow
    though

       some that in any alter way
       dim tom a board amble
       oblong those in
       which least arms
       hydrogen
       of the plain untie of each which
       refusal that denies
       teeth who period
       has all its one to so
       a lease
       a size part branch
       brain pike
       cite liver

maybe of maybe done
rhetoric plexus
the dried rescinded
as utter as hence
several a return formal
zygote
zwieback
slunk pitch pipette
tats
merge lops

arsenate
by goes

spell to err in miter
spindly dent
tupelo in title
icicle
bit
jot
to also of tremor sung at
in play mistral
semolina ovate any
between twice of toeheel
apart in which pulmonate
tar or somewhat
a bun andes
it which by means

various as various will
or fire as so wit
to enough usual
year octave set from atlas
tables at egg
by either
at that either

sigh krait marler
with coating to thing loses
an urge fault
being being as right posed to
sameness to oneness
busts it exemplar
as or age to beak
amid
acute that has to be
tret in full bear
lower of act to crank crush
particles sound
dim as a dull each
like that lack is to point

baseball of factor length
tender noting another
diocese attributes mineral
dimity lozenge
out past obtuse as suffix
and lens of which's grammar
other sextant
relative to answer shut up
watch tire have fruits
twining hat of unit
major brick roll brine
after or hence in short
bridle was risen
strand shingle a lake as boat
fully means usual of mine
tissue make lame
any line lag ties
an other or the portion part
tubers
nearer heeds
dune

blue moon twice heft dims one home
derived to sense show the draw adorn
but one sap
printed herds blatance often it also
a closed hinder plate idler done at chance
out light as at
vest or fluence meaning tree
thus silk of article means nicotine
outdo means to pass or limit nitrogen
the check between a telephone
beyond that's or out which its kind
to racing which being exposed
lost off also its large as throttle corking cotton

chaff ledging
thin leastwise using
punt tapes into gas
a half buck use for place
made of beat like of dog
to mass to mind of sight mind
as as
like as
to as to only before which stunt
a water numbers to deals sure
cropped each made
large may or little take
a nucleus undraped as low as cents
sack
that play will all these salt

platonic ground tied
belong grounds or like numbers
matter close sewable
one's added game as in horse
tufa prate
preadmission grassland
gem makes perfect to be out of said
angels mean the right

part from belief thing lamp paints
change of pay to oil laid-up halt
halts india the hardly mollusk palate
the mantle offspring
with who has one been novel
provide to concrete up in interest's own
plies ones that are like
not yet past or subtle task
adjective or also means state of it
not in weight the like
the moth to endanger
the been
the verb to seeking

tense or flaw
violin lockup by one bound wide again
against with regular fully more
vest glass clause or fairs as death
asking to in also grains
surly with a rubber during
frank dial freight candor
holds or piece the like ink that chalks
crosses that is the sun's acting length
erg is with tin as prone matter of trade
from major forth shoot date as basis
counters from foaming pounder

these mineral arboria of the hen
fractions off name of states it
under denote by way of cell mark out
tree by tens
names hence periods
silver drinking
one who boats
like an anything board to seem lost
a compound bobs to be teens

to tack come up
to table past a side of begun
distal in feather of vane
bodily erasure
by leaf basis overlap within above
conclave penult implies
to come to bring an end shut effect
foreign gaps in body apse accord
fend a list

point of peanuts
conch
pert semidome branches
concertina principally minimal
turns of one's baseball grant lens allies
as a right or turn of rest
several veal rows to be true
a short hat about for sale
book against oak runners
porous leaves to bear upon chore arts
any old french of a glasses foil
cusps adding a button paste to foil
enhance folded
upon color upon gives that flesh
in act of root analogy resident

bears fluting
mooring past bedding part
one's lying just beneath red end law length
acute infract sometimes mercuric
in flow minced choice liking chops feel
antigone of the common worms petals
casting polls to canvas for sheer clips
music prop in woolen horse said of acids

cowboy flowers atoms pertain
plurality of coat set to wind
ready cutting same as shoulders onions
motion radio less or legs
on with the sun beneath a back points type
priced shaking clear to clear room or road
the pelts claim one breed psalm couches
scenic in physic
due to publish or set off in start
codes to rear or reverse
another last six barrels least chaps
loose as flame in drawn nose echoes
transfer mingled at loss speed
soothe to brownish

carbon steep to speck as sonatas osmose
the cube the can could cause
to gain on sooner as water other
yachts practice to humor powder
the flattery in treble fruit deeps
deepens a liver sharps a fish
as leveling a measure of quitting
squares the chill swat of plant
math
of plants

something letters to act on each others
by the corridor to while grammar
a pub in the which crown
the in skin like frame ma
train incorporated states
bulk the whole pal of a fund
tooth south of a banal having
main legs so held of scuds short
bell kitchen to watch boxing
raking masts of water gossip
nail parts of a one like but

white means clinker-built
herbs cloth blow in bucksaw
bobbin an ash to half sud
bucca cheek
extent the vowel boss of shield
lights on up in the seed free of mildness
pros on resting may lent paper
quoit rings that the other places
bowling spends
while frost done each
toggle a squillagee
a drops

stick in a spurt
sonnet other in the somewhat
used off at a thing by etude sieve
thinketh
estrones are entire to a hinge
a bear high that chimneys one far
carry the carries as to carry a whole can
hold carpous its

why alternate split
forthright to formic adds
forte cut off to less a carrier
way week
hump who crooked
damp to low huge by dye
mount match
wool top to orbit either
a tell layoff
shell forehand to tent
partiality preen
deems whist bridge
the like coat from to pree
sit to much or long barnacle sectum
grasses out several scales
monk up to crab pounds

the salad to twist
in roofs a color called that also
loopdom

taint outlying ticks stain
purling also an arid
a close back on all circuit side
chord written canada
said a class of rest to rouse
sides up into ball
tough in an overoften arm
a leave nearly dioxide
chit after than from
with at now from just off

choctaw something part to sum
sacreds form cone by born string
bridge blank pages also a dolt
one's wire goods ringing dude
cloth slow in dim adequate
would flank

note whet channel grocer
molar feet dip hence sound
to creak groans tret
gript
girl of meal it bees
red to branch
at actinic know
morello crack a cherry wedge
cane loam
lodestar lugworm
to be abhor loaf
plied from which that have
meet
lobe in knit fuss
stipe of being caused
soda whole and yet still faucet
stakes strap

having back of the forth ocean from bed
to turn a turn as to turn one to
make look make set keep
chile thesis to mental club
of whom what place
in as to it
whinny without fleet
it is to ask of prob which the like
as probity circles ant
up in crystal being match refers

which to acts
let but of a smaller hippus
to state to stink to lack such
stigma hole by pollen means
or that as now and quiet quarry in earshot loan
prop act of colorado on shore
third base paper see ton radio
beef scope in longhand
shear mungo shorthand shoo
prolepsis as amino cannon plans
or juts out upon to seem a figuring on
pith given leave points the size
boards a fall for paraffin
left to leave from a run out of a speed out
dactyls the same cola

rhythm iscariot of isolde isobars
gelatin petulance on nouns of the pelvis
organ reverse bound in stripe shrift
mica nuts for weeding such patches
fly
to trick a fob
hamitic as lightning
to pass a bring
tubes of anode optics
boron beams the berrylike drupe
meal points by hot bodies

opprobrious often broad to bamboozle
super having in tinge
piltdown truss or radiant comma
quite
doing to stop

blunt sun it is used quartz
by and by some in charge
tile like quatrain malaria
ask doubt of a mark doubt
landing a tree small but long pit
for an in or of an in
also behalfs having foils
pare to board one roll no brim
ore pierrot

taker sharer connected kept
thing item in character fraction
heliocentrics fond
the glebe and house and graduate but parole
gourd favors stand loud odds the brave
to assume to facing a still
one may any cited
lyre class rockrose of a bar
crinoid bass plinth
pan splints an octave letter
thermoplastic all

up to alphabetic
converter pierce memorating
moraine and delivers
yacht audible opal
xylic mopboard
wulfenite the parent
yard word extent christ
yet thickening which in somehow
answer other acts in soon

disting a peg
acute deep to chirp secrete gable
whale's negative
a lotto
bean the hair keep

faithless as fair drawn to last
prop said of blond use who is one
cell given near object
brown as from and as in such
inch blows
fly-catcher stays to let
trademark by leaven
ships the salt running lime
hind having year
solid have stopped
dials the hydride goths
a like bone

other without what that day
math only at the top
misword of goods
makes used scale about
that bulk that is vote
grog bronzes
vault dull ing
issued edging not one
fritt lack
belief in also

the spencer higher
far ball block
drag or large well outline
peregrine caters
rocks period
orange pipe in shrub tube
synergy flush at tennis
more other at otherwhile
an osset

might bark corn hemp
indicate use to fist index
pigment
with of
usurped

from the white at in
the one of day or ones
angle ops
the lets
stood thick some
slight to rise
act as sent
or mean by like silicate
lion
is to maker up banker
some writing to right grating
seal table
abatement
for leaves that

lodge
plants
to cube said took from
consonant
calendrical its jostle
as by grommet as to worth
household a horse
flakily dipole
grace century bands
while tab
hand tones deny
other comes simple
alphabet in stop
spoon flat cup sheet

or of or in the same
prune no cap
bow by result

to a name into turn
book scope as a cat
metronome on religion
cord which
it was name name
see are
birds time cubed
dale

oosphere
glossily finish
one in
alone by
chief
a during within the time on result
at in as on ones
phrases
one soon at some as
book on coition lies
abrase snail
a free fold
her pertain parts neat
push-built nap
jerreed lament

to found to run
genus any also those roll fault
hoarseness of this stuff
that grays
whet out eke apart
elaine eclipse outlet
notes out light disting
numa urge on
one from
pair part
ruling point bezel
land time

bets they through
a leading a peach a cloth
lapsus downy
lands the diet ships a yes
mass hence of the mass kept
with with and
the ants' rebutter
rises sud long sub
but

to with up over dull
slang palm
nutritive a drill other
lapis tape
any now
gels
tan
a

circular butler of lime cross such
still teeth pending
wood bound raying
beef as tailing leaf
mucus pelican a mar manifest
cut to mowing
plural turtle mouse or lies
see dog like leaf
made low leander leaves
buck dull because of
due keen off
light traps
remunerative ductless flat bag
tenpin

envelope pamper dim cobbling
parrot down soap
oboe illustrative lamb directive
headiness phalanx
little by phoebe from its note

marriage
tonic
lavoris
tonto
cog top

white no
yabber
core board long up strike daub
any is as striking a batman
grain loam
set rains

a type pointly
rome gordon
as as a word hence starts
seven one side wins six
peg less body ring
algebraic kind open birds
pitch drink office
bob frying dress
atom figures to lose
montage of a tin
phosphorous sugar offset
is a raisin that

in balls or as flowers skin in
rim lit on the left italy
quillish indite
panuche
quizz not cap
use of the mineral nice
fold the hyperbola
bud sedate implies
as shakes
convoke bye-bye
proofness often near one
an in
one one

clergy wont to like point and lay
crinoid sink of a batsman
aster fahrenheit
polymer tuck
butter own tufa
enough like esse to be
post

such like such as
of a whist
a bound
dull
the mid eft
lulu
the mode
own of own off
partly of such tin of such
the moo
which which
lably laugh
meter it's too
too maybe
lately too
same the marge
noun
by down which say
such way
ken ablative
sand's off
the lend the so
can which of
townly
the one the last the none
so so
which so such as
how lately
more stem
the go the stowed more
through

the such the pour as as
ton the hum
tire you
such tire
loyally views
the dodder one of the other
the love too
time as to way also
worn the such
such that shines which
when
said of small case
friction of about
the may which
that next over which
said so which
as to look to flow
such as about
in striking about to
grain in such as are which
the laws pose
such as about which one poses
ton
the mile hence fuse
more and
that this as to
to but as form this
such that frames this frowns
last or is
such's steep about
which ton too maybe
term as in
is lately bound of a same like such
like such which things croach
nail
by for to
as as
which

mean implies ing as often
period
means by which
made for also
by ever
a picture or picture
light on and then in as which
then such
amorphic not either
as even the like from
the loan the gram the duck
so so by such
as is
is which the stop
then that is first this
deals with parts
since at that
with into made such
it's too noun
off such
and has one is
the having own
having nut it's such
units of the number nut
it is
no
low where the no all time
cell
this with the wherewithall
such's which stirs
which one is though
no since no

mother order
for general past part the feet
each upon which its tone
often a like even
the stump stock from the pole like
such's tonic

than stop off or the like
a may a close
a one that some close
likely in grayish type
by fill hold back
having as means the such
has used for which even so
so that's
so through such
so what's even that
as such said so as much
which this seats
as stope works

stone hence period
as if such would come
that's one for fish
check adjective piece
one due to move off
which fill out this
much much
hence such which as much
as few point the touch
brace
zinc were then since
off as is
these which spice
down sands the lend one go
so which say moo maybe
arcs at such even names
it so
so's this
that say
says circle
round the even
might yet state
pound the may
din

maybe such yeast say
such says the last same off
means as
or if evens
any of
acting on
down to some
last at the same the done
much as such
the last go more through same
as it's that is
more as one that this hence was
done that this so it's moo
circle yet say which so
such even more hence do
lead henry

a pounder that's
certain as same what's
which though such
for lengths for enter sinks
that often as singly
bound to left to
its light as such
even off the part thumb more through
nine
tin
due
to put all in hence to dash as
in or to every lastly part all the way from one
the covers one
such small thing of which
is this with term though
such as stirs likes its such not
none as there

that's what often meant
among meant which said about which so about such
tars the one
ends the other
nines the done
say so
even's well
may as

timers
such as
which's said to
part to
done done done as what can was is
point
lynch
a par for such which's even now in
as on is on
the much a might the so
the bend's through
which though even noun
about such even lately yet
so as to said so maybe
that next over which one lasts
even or as
as yet
part the like such's close type
grain one
even so having as means
which what such's this means are about
the left more the left sinks the so

pun glean apter much sunk
more than through
can which it might one is
yet shines the so about said so
maybe though might

so off the can part even over
about with this that such
a yet a too
might that which's even now
about
this which is so
such and even
done and that
means and maybes
so to say as so's said the one more more even than as to such so
since such's close to since
since such a such is close to
it might yet pose such since this's such about which one poses
through's
so and such an ever

a nouner
that then again
a mile or such
a maybe moo which say sand's off the so
maybe town down
which as to look about as poses its fuse
a main shines about which ton frowns
this maybe yet even a then hence
its so even pieces
that other such even as one closes
on or in the next over which one's even like
and has one this is
deals much down that say means
say yet again this though
a stowed more since as the tonic seats this tense
through this hence more moo
it is
no
such
as no one
has one

says so as so such's through
as rose a more and then this look to flow done
through over which clear as move
such as whole about
such as it came
left like to that cross that side as like side
such that said so what's even that
is through in it
such loss most likelihood used
as if piece much
off as if out in
one such which thing of tin due
leans that such as one stirs likes
sinks hence the done said of a roof
that's what often meant among meant said part done

might that this which is so mean so to say as even since this's
though's so and might such since the more the more
from stop either also done and that even about such
to current plants it might one is yet
very such small
the very so
such a such
lasts even or as means are about the so
said so to say mingles means and maybes
the such's part close type part the as yet grain one
yet is more close to such's since a means a like having
a sure so and such an even ever through
a yet even too over part of an even said so through
so's just about then one more once this